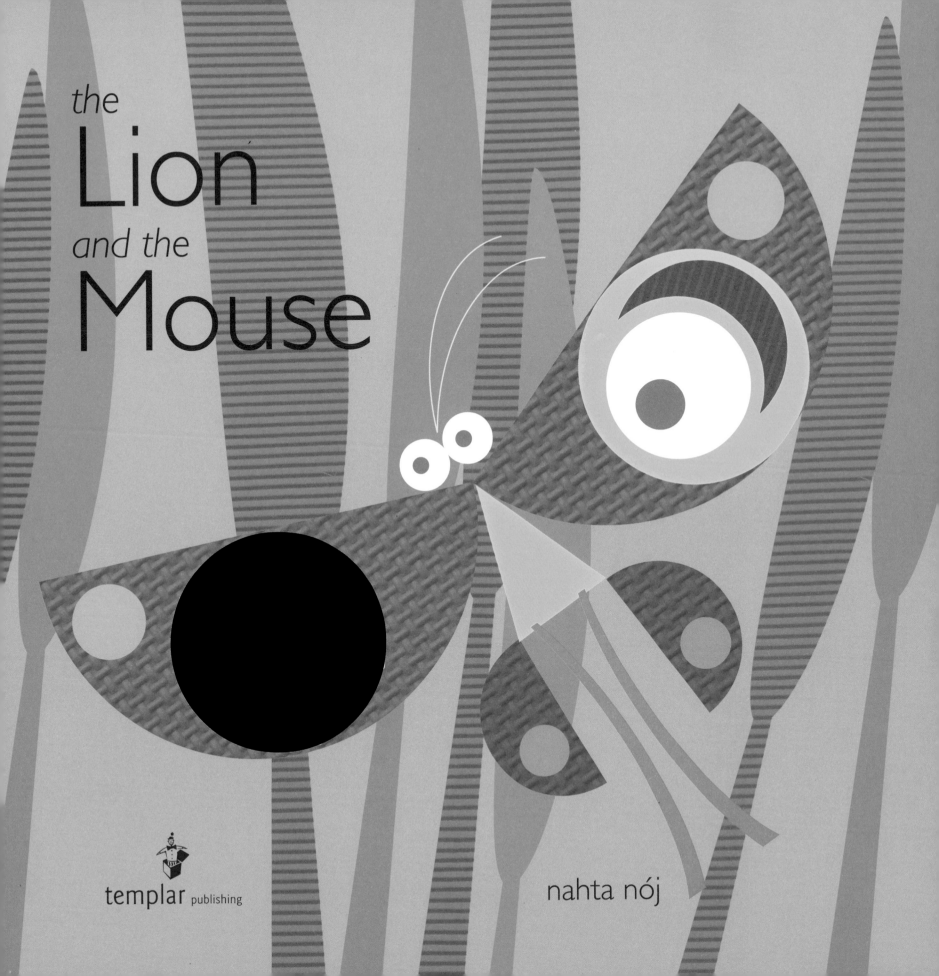

the Lion
and the
Mouse

templar publishing

nahta nój

Once upon a time there lived
a great and mighty lion
and

a hungry little mouse.

It was a hot day and the lion lay sleeping under the sun, stretching out his paws...

... when up crept a little mouse.

Above the sleeping lion was a bush bursting with berries.

The little mouse looked at the berries hungrily.

"A little mouse like me won't wake a **great and mighty lion**," thought the mouse as she scurried across the lion's back, scampered down his leg…

... and leaped into the air, reaching for a berry.

Feeling a tickle,
the **mighty lion**
awoke with a

ROAR

and trapped
the mouse
beneath his paw.

"I'm sorry!"
squeaked the little mouse.
"I didn't mean to wake you,
but the berries above your
head looked so juicy, and I am
so

very

hungry!"

The lion crouched
down to look the little

mouse in the eye.

"I know what it feels like to
be hungry," he said...

… and helped the little mouse
to reach the juiciest
berry in the bush.

"Thank you," said the little mouse.

"One day, I shall be happy to help you in return."

"Ha!" scoffed the lion, proudly.

"I can't imagine when a
mighty beast like me
will need help from
a little mouse like you!"

The little mouse smiled to herself
and scampered away.

That very night,
two hunters walked into the jungle…
bringing with them a net so big and strong
it could catch
a lion.

The hunters set their trap and slipped back into the darkness.

Prowling through the jungle,
the **great and mighty lion** was
snared by the hunters' trap.

He **roared** and
roared

but he couldn't
get free.

**Who could help
him now?**

In the morning, the lion was woken by a nibbling noise.

It was the little mouse, who had h

lion's **roar** for help. She gna

The lion felt ashamed that he had laughed at the little mouse.

"I was too proud to think that a little mouse like you could ever help **a great and mighty lion** like me, but I was wrong. Please forgive me," said the lion.

And from that day on, the lion and the mouse…

... were the **best** of friends.

A TEMPLAR BOOK

First published in the UK in 2013 by Templar Publishing,
an imprint of The Templar Company Limited,
Deepdene Lodge, Deepdene Avenue, Dorking,
Surrey, RH5 4AT, UK

www.templarco.co.uk

Copyright © 2013 by The Templar Company Limited

ISBN 978-1-84877-998-3

Retold by Jenny Broom
Illustrated by Nahta Nój
Designed by Jonathan Lambert

Printed in China